THE BAD MOTHER

Published by Dymaxicon
An imprint of Agile Learning Labs
San Francisco, CA

First Edition
ISBN 978-0-9828669-0-0

www.dymaxicon.com

The text of this book is set in Calluna by Jos Bivuenga
Titles are set in Downcome by Eduardo Recife

THE BAD MOTHER

a novel by

Nancy Rommelmann

DYMAXICON

CHAPTER ONE

Sitting on the toilet, Mary ran her fingers over the tiny blister. She thought maybe she'd given it to herself from scratching so much, but it was another one of those sores. At the clinic, they'd given her a tube of special cream, but Dean had used it up the night before.

"I need that," she'd told him. She was on the mattress in the middle of the loft, running her hand over her belly as she watched him in the bathroom, squeezing a line of cream down his penis.

"Yea, well," he said, "I need it, too."

"But the doctor said if I don't use it and I get one, the baby can be born retarded."

"Yea, well, fuck the baby, these things itch like mother fuckers." He made little circles with the cream. "These doctors don't know what they're talking about, anyway. How's a baby, who's been in his mother's stomach for nine months, going to get retarded just by touching it?"

Mary didn't know, so she didn't say anything. She watched him inspect some dry patches on his hipbones. He dabbed what was left of the cream on these, too, though Mary thought they looked like something else, pimples that had never opened up, just healed over.

"Baby?" Dean said, looking at her with enough of a smile, waiting.

Mary pushed herself off the mattress. Dirt stuck to her feet as she walked to the bathroom. The bulb over the sink was making Dean's skin the color of a rotten apple, and the whites of his eyes popped in a scary way, so Mary concentrated on looking for the irregular gold flecks in his dark eyes. Like lion's eyes, she thought. Dean brought his nose almost to hers and closed his eyes on purpose.

Mary laid her cheek on Dean's chest and waited for him to tug on what was left of her bangs, cut the week before with nail scissors. Waited while her thumbs trapped the hairs on his stomach. She held onto his waistband as he pushed down on her shoulders; one kneecap smacked on the tile.

She wanted to sound sweet, to say "Let me see," but Dean gripped her jaw and pushed in. The slickness of the cream covered her teeth. She was careful

not to scrape the heads off the sores, imagining they
tasted like salt water inside.

CHAPTER TWO

Mary always woke up when the buses started rolling down Hollywood Boulevard, not from the noise coming in the windows, but the exhaust. It had been worse in the beginning; the best she'd been able to do was to lie on the mattress with her jean jacket over her face and will herself not to puke. One time Dean bought her a pack of cherry Rolaids, and MeeMee mixed a drink she swore was a cure brought over by slaves, which turned out to be Nestea and vodka and which MeeMee drank most of anyway. At the clinic they told Mary it would get easier after three months.

The day they told her she was pregnant, she'd sat under the swings in Poinsettia Park and crunched handfuls of wet sand. She wanted to be mad at Leather, to somehow get him on a pay phone in San Francisco and tell him she was not safer in Los

Angeles—look what had happened. Who knew if Leather was still around anyway; his hand had trembled so much it took him three tries to get the $80 into her shirt pocket at her mom's wake in the park. He told Mary, with his grape-smelling breath, that they couldn't put her in services if they couldn't find her, and LA was a good town for a kid on her own, way warmer than on the Bay.

Mary knew this was not always true; her butt got numb from sitting in the wet sand. But when she stepped off the bus six months ago there'd been a warm wind that smelled a little like fire and also the warmth from the bus idling as it let off passengers. People got out of parked cars and took other people's suitcases and said, "*Hola,*" and then the cars pulled away. The bus backed up and drove away. Mary didn't think the station would be open so late, but it was, even if all the ticket windows were shut and there was no one inside except a man in coveralls who didn't say anything about the bathrooms being locked. He watched Mary try the door, and then said he'd unlock it for her but she had to leave her knapsack with him.

"Why?" Mary asked.

"Because I don't know what you're going to do in there." He sounded mad at her, but Mary thought it was probably because some accident had scooped out a big part of his neck and face, an acne-purple scar that sent a shock through Mary's genitals. She told him he could hold it, but her mom's ashes were in there so he had to be careful.

Mary had not been back to the bus station, but had seen the man one other time, slowing as he passed the theater across from the loft, stopping in front of a poster of a woman smiling and offering her gigantic boobs on a platter. From the way the woman's hair was styled, Mary knew the poster was old and that the woman was not performing in that club, if she ever had been. But the man with the bad neck had brought his face right up close to the poster, and Mary, standing in the glass entry-way of the electronic store, saw him sniff it before continuing east on Hollywood. Mary didn't know the real name of the theater manager, they just called him the Dwarf, but she wondered what he'd think of a man smelling his poster, and if she should mention it, but she probably wouldn't, because even though she saw the Dwarf propped on a stool under the marquee every afternoon, all he ever said to her and her friends was, "Move it. Move it."

The theater was about the last place you'd want to sit, anyway. The best place was by the IHOP; after a big breakfast the tourists were inclined to give you the change they'd just been given. But the IHOP was all the way on the other side of La Brea, plus no one wanted to get up early, so mostly Mary just hung out across the street at the Falafel King.

"Roll up your shirt," Dean would say, scooting close to her on the flattened-out box, putting a consoling palm on Mary's knee or stroking her hair while keeping his eyes on the passing tourists. Sitting cross-legged on the corner of Hollywood and Wilcox, the take-out box at her feet, she'd turn her face to the sun and listen to what the world dropped in.

CHAPTER THREE

The week Mary was due, Sofia ordered the guys to help clean up the loft. Face-down on the mattress by the window, Dean pretended to be asleep, and when Sofia shook him, he swatted up and caught his nail on her cheekbone.

"You asshole," she said, holding her cheek.

"You shouldn't be waking people up like that." Dean grabbed his shirt off the floor and sat with his back to the rest of them.

"You still have to help," Sofia said, checking her fingers for blood.

Sitting on the orange sofa they'd dragged from outside the Lido apartments, Mary watched Dean leave the loft without saying goodbye. Only she, Sofia and Roach were left, MeeMee having been busted again the day before for lifting a bra-and-panty set from downstairs at Playmates. Sofia and Roach picked up bottles and cans and handed them to Mary, who placed them in the garbage bag between her feet.

"About three dollars' worth, I'd say," Roach said, spinning the bag shut and volunteering to use the rebate to do laundry, something Mary had never heard a guy do. The girls were always hauling the towels and motel bedspreads and various articles of black clothing to the Wash-o-Mat on Cahuenga. Mary had been watching the loads go round-and-round a few weeks ago when a fight broke out, two Mexican guys with broken bottles jabbing at each other outside the doorway. There'd been no place for her to go, and she hadn't felt safe, not with the baby coming. After she'd pushed the cart full of clean stuff back to the loft, she'd told Dean about the fight. He'd been on an afternoon drunk and yelled he was going to kick some spic ass as he crashed out the door, then he didn't come back until the next afternoon.

"It's no problem. I used to do washing for my mom." Roach pushed his dark blond hair back from a tan forehead. They all had tans, those who didn't cultivate the white-death look. Mary thought Roach didn't look as though he'd been on the streets longer than a few weeks, though he told her it had been two years. She'd been with him twice, when she first came to Hollywood, and both times had been nice; he didn't pound her or pull her hair back. Now he was sixteen, and Mary could see the split seam in his t-shirt as he hoisted the bottles over one shoulder, the laundry over the other.

Roach had the best intentions and made the five-minute walk to the Wash-o-Mat in just under forty-five, stopping first to blow a joint with Top Jimmy, whose left foot was looking worse.

"Kind of green now, ain't it?" Roach asked, looking at a dark circle that had seeped through Jimmy's sock.

Top Jimmy made a point of not looking at his foot when anyone else was around, but he could picture it, having examined it under the freeway overpass the night before, using brown paper towels he took from the Falafel King's bathroom to carefully soak and peel off the bandages. They'd been dark yellow with puss, but the foot underneath wasn't green—that was just the dirt on the sock he kept over it—it was red and open, and still bled if he banged it by accident. The lady at the runaway center said he needed to take the antibiotics she gave him, but he'd sold them as X to some kids from the Valley or somewhere. Jimmy figured they'd snuck out of the Mann's Chinese while the film was on, their folks sitting in the dark with their fists in jumbo popcorns, because how else did these kids with braces and $100 gym shoes get to Hollywood?

Jimmy didn't have a shoe for his bad foot. He'd had to slice up his old one more and more as his foot swelled and finally he chucked it altogether. He'd thought about getting a crutch, which might earn him extra cash, but he had to find one first. He wondered where those winos got their crutches.

"It's not as bad as it looks," he told Roach. "You washing?"

Roach nodded and handed the roach to Jimmy. Jimmy stuck it between his teeth and pulled his black sweatshirt and t-shirt over his head and stuffed them in Roach's garbage bag. Top Jimmy's skin was translucent; Roach could see each of the ribs, which looked like branches under a frozen pond. He began imagining one of them straining against then snapping though Jimmy's skin, the tip sticking out clean, or no, it would bleed. It would bleed, right? Roach figured this was the pot and looked up the boulevard.

It was 10:30, still early, though the tourists were out and dressed for the day. They thought their pastels worked perfectly in the California sun, but they were in Hollywood, not Malibu, so their clothes looked like vomit on the sparkling gray sidewalks. They stopped every few feet, the women's knee flab sagging over the stars of yesteryear, the husbands balancing camcorders on their guts and gaping at the store windows full of whore's clothes. They deliberately did not look at Roach, though their kids did; they stared and stared until they were herded on by the mothers, their faces panicked at the possibility of

Roach asking for a quarter. He never did ask; these people weren't real, more like slow-moving figures in a video game.

Not to say Roach didn't take some interest. He let his eyes linger on the small girls, the shy girls, girls bland as mice, girls who looked like boys. He could spend all day walking La Brea to Vine with a girl visiting from Victoria, Canada; a girl with a guidebook and a knapsack who bought him lunch; a girl with whom the possibility of sex faded early, leaving them free to sneak through the fence behind the wax museum, goof off in the wig shops and record stores, and effortlessly drift apart come dusk—Roach was always grateful to the ones who didn't push to stay until night—he accepting though not really wanting her copy of *Siddhartha*.

Most American girls weren't like that. They spent their half-day on the boulevard trying to prove they belonged, leading with their chins, wearing tiny neon clothes that made belly-rolls and shouting, "Oh, shit!" every few feet. Roach could see and hear these girls coming from blocks away; they were no more annoying than the buses letting out big farts of exhaust, and they could usually be counted on to provide a joint, a slice of pizza, five bucks. Dean would tell these girls he'd get them some fine pot, then leave Roach making small talk. They didn't seem to mind that Dean never came back. But what did these girls think? That he was going to treasure the scraps of paper they'd written their phone numbers on?

"You want me to buy you something to eat?" Roach asked, but Top Jimmy shook his head. Roach took off up Cahuenga.

Next to the laundry was a 7-Eleven, and next to that the Hollywood 8 Motel. In the morning the motel was quiet, since most of the people who got rooms stayed up all night smoking crack. Roach knew Miralee stayed there when she had money. After he traded in the bottles ("No trade for these," the 7-Eleven guy said, fishing Top Jimmy's shirts out of the bag) and got the laundry going, he used some quarters to buy an orange juice and a milk, and went up to the black grate security door of the motel.

The lady who ran the motel was from India. She had a husband, but Roach heard he'd been shot. She didn't allow visitors, but she knew Roach, who sometimes pulled her dumpsters onto the street for five bucks.

"Did that girl with the baby come last night?" Roach asked.

The Indian woman nodded. "Same room," she said, and buzzed Roach in. "Wait."

Roach stood in the concrete breezeway while the woman went into the tiny office. She came back holding something wrapped in waxed paper that looked like a soggy turnover. She handed it to Roach.

"Thanks," he said, holding the samosa as if it were a bomb and heading up to 202.

CHAPTER FOUR

Sofia was on her knees scrubbing the bathtub. Sweat was making the back of her neck itch and she knew her hair was frizzing. "You can do it in water, you know."

"I don't know about that." Mary was sitting on the closed toilet seat, digging into the pocket of her army pants.

Sofia saw Mary's zipper had ripped all the way out. "What happened to those sweats I gave you?"

"I don't know." She pulled out a flattened pack of Marlboro Lights and held it out to Sofia, who shook her head and went back to the tub. There was work to do; she wanted to be ready, in case Mary had the baby in the loft, which she thought was very possible, since the guy who first brought Sofia up here hadn't been back in two months. He said he was an

Israeli photographer who used the loft as a studio and promised her $150 an hour if she'd pose. After the session, which ended with Sofia riding the guy on a rust-stained mattress, he'd told her to wait while he went to the ATM. But Sofia figured she was getting the better end of the deal because the only person who ever showed up after that was an exterminator.

"Seriously, I saw this TV show where the minute the baby is born, it can swim," she said. "And it doesn't need to breathe yet because it hasn't been breathing the whole time it's in the mother, so water is its natural environment."

"I don't think Dean would go for the water part." Mary blew smoke rings. "He's pretty traditional."

"Oh, he's fucking Abe Lincoln. Crap." Sofia sucked her teeth as she tried to pull her fingers through her hair. It was hard to keep any kind of conditioner around, with so many people in and out of the loft. Once she'd hidden a bottle of Pantene in her sleeping bag and it was gone by that night.

Sofia didn't so much care that people went through her stuff; it was sort of flattering. Sofia knew she was destined to be famous; sometimes she sat on the window ledge overlooking Hollywood Boulevard, one bare leg hanging out like a girl in a Sprite commercial, and watched the limos—she liked the white ones—thinking that eventually the tinted back window of this or that car would roll down and an older guy, maybe a little bald but that would be okay, would smile up at her and say, "Want to go for a ride?" And it wouldn't be just for sex, it would be because he was a big producer of music videos and she was exactly the kind of girl he was looking to make into a star, and also to be his girlfriend, because she was prettier than the other girls he'd been with, and also because, he'd tell her, she had a purity that he didn't want to see wasted. Soon after meeting this man, Sofia would insist Mary live with them in his big house, and the man would say, of course, and give her $10,000 in hundreds to get what she needed for herself and Mary and the baby. Then the girls would sit together on a ruffled bed with a canopy and listen to Sofia's new CDs on a stereo built into the wall, next to a white wicker bookshelf full of stuffed animals and a big clean window letting in the sun and overlooking a garden with one of those mazes they make out of hedges.

"Can we get food?" asked Mary.

Sofia'd been on her knees so long her legs were pins and needles. "You have money?"

"Two dollars."

"That'll do you but not me." Sofia dropped the sponge into the half-cleaned tub and pulled off her sweaty tank top. She patted cold water from the sink on her chest and under her arms.

"Early for a date," Mary said.

"Not really." Sofia looked at Mary's t-shirt, hot pink with the sleeves and neck cut off. "Can I use that? I got nothing."

Mary pulled off the shirt.

"Whoa," Sofia said. "Why are your nipples black?"

Mary looked down at her boobs; they were pointing straight out like little torpedoes. "I don't know," she said, and dug in her pocket to get a single and some change. "Just bring me whatever."

Sofia leaned into the mirror and wiped her teeth with her finger. "Wear a towel or something until Roach gets back. Some freak might come up and you don't want to be naked."

CHAPTER FIVE

Roach heard Freddy groan. "Who is it?"

"It's Roach. Lemme in"

Roach waited a long time for Miralee to open the door. Her eyes were puffy and her mango-colored hair was wedged on one side of her head. "Hey, Roach."

Roach could tell it was the first thing she'd said this morning when her breath hit him, but it was okay. He liked Miralee.

The motel room was dark and felt dirty. The stroller was in the corner, next to a tall pack of Pampers ripped open and toppled over. Freddy was in bed without a shirt on, waving out the match he'd used to light the first cigarette of the day.

"What'd you bring us?"

Roach held up the juice. He watched Miralee, in

a t-shirt and panties, fumble through the crumpled cigarette packs and ash and trash on the bedside table.

Roach looked for the baby, and saw she was in the bathroom, on her toes, hanging onto the sink, trying to put a pink plastic ladies razor in her mouth. He walked in and took the razor out of her hand. She looked at him, babbled something, and got on her hands and knees and crawled. She was big, but she didn't walk yet, Miralee said from being in the stroller so much. And that's where she went, climbing in by herself as her mother lit the empty glass pipe.

"Shit. You got anything to get us going, Roach?"

Roach shook his head.

"Then what are you doing here?" Miralee flopped back on the bed and stared at the ceiling, though Roach knew she wasn't really mad; who the hell had anything left in the morning? He sat at the end of the bed near Miralee's foot and felt a throb start beneath his collarbones, and a pulse in the inches between him and Miralee. Roach liked looking at her big brown eyes set far apart like a calf's and long eyelashes that always looked wet, as though she rubbed her whole eye area with Vaseline. Roach noticed she wore men's t-shirts, maybe to hide her big chest, but her legs you could always see, taut and golden in her cutoffs. She reminded Roach of one of those Hawaiian surfer chicks you see on TV, as though she should be running along the beach with jungle flowers in her hair instead of standing on the street with an eighteen-month-old kid and a thirty-year-old husband.

Freddy was dark, missing his front teeth, and way too skinny from the crack. Roach heard he'd been on the streets a long time, but he was not getting mellow like some of the old-timers. Once he smacked MeeMee for saying he was old enough to be Miralee's daddy, right there on the corner of Yucca and Wilcox by the Pla-Boy Liquor Mart, which, with all the cops around, was the last place you wanted to get loud. But Freddy didn't care, just smacked MeeMee in the mouth when she said it, like you would a little kid. She put her fingers to her lip, then grabbed Freddy's collar and began slapping at his head until he pulled a short knife, and she screamed so loud Top Jimmy had to put his hand over her mouth and tell her to shut up, shut up.

Roach watched the whole thing from the corner of Yucca and Cahuenga, standing with Miralee, the baby in the stroller at her knee. Two squad cars pulled around the corner, sirens on. Everyone took their hands off whomever they were grabbing and did the innocent, look-at-the-ground thing. Freddy was going for his bike when a cop pushed him face-first to the wall of the liquor-mart and patted him down, and when he found the knife asked, "What's this?" MeeMee said, "That's right," and when the cop asked if she had something to say, she said, "Just that this motherfucker tried to stab me," at which point Freddy called her a greasy nigger cunt and spit, so that the cop wrenched Freddy's arm behind his back, pushed him down on the sidewalk and put a knee in his back. He read him his rights and cuffed him while MeeMee screamed she was going to fuck up his greasy-ass motherfucking Mexican ass, until this other cop planted his hand on her chest and told her she needed to "cool down."

"You want to take a walk?" Miralee had asked Roach. She'd already started pushing the stroller. Roach walked her to the Hollywood 8, where she pulled twenty singles out of the baby's bag and tried to get the night manager to let them in. He shook his head and said, "Twenty-six," which meant Miralee had to stand in front of the 7-Eleven. Roach stood off to the side because he didn't want to hurt her chances; that, and he was embarrassed someone would think it was his kid. It took only ten minutes for Miralee to get three dollars—Roach already had three—plus a carton of milk for the baby and a tub of Ben & Jerry's some old stoner bought her. Miralee complained they always took in more milk and diapers than she could use, and that the 7-Eleven guys wouldn't let her cash them in anymore. She stood in the motel breezeway looking up at the balcony, and told Roach he could come up, if he wanted. They smoked a little pot that Roach had stashed in his sock and ate the ice cream on the bed, Miralee feeding fingerfuls to the baby. Then she turned out the light and let Roach run his hands over the outside of her shirt, and told him of her plan to get an address so she could start the welfare checks coming again.

It had been the first night in a long time Roach remembered dreaming. He was with Miralee, in front of a small white farmhouse up north, on one of those country roads that wind off into the distance. It was before dawn, just a red-gold strip at the horizon. They were lying on a small patch of plowed dirt. Not nasty dirt, but clean warm russet dirt. Roach breathed in, the life in the dirt streaming up his nostrils and depositing fine grit on his palate. He pinched the dirt between his fingers, knowing the red stain it would leave. He placed one hand on the warm ground as the other reached for Miralee. When he woke up in the dark motel room, he could still smell the wet wood of the earth, and pretended it might linger for the next breath while knowing it would not. He looked at Miralee. She was facing him, sleeping with her mouth open, showing a space where she'd lost a tooth; the baby was on a blanket on the floor, curled into a ball. Roach thought it must be early, and quietly opened the door in order not to wake the girls, and was surprised the sun was directly overhead, since the manager was usually banging on everyone's door by ten.

"If you didn't bring us rock, how about food?" Miralee asked. She cringed as Roach handed her the milk, poured it into a yellowed plastic bottle for the baby, and lay back with her arm over her eyes.

"Sunny out there?" she asked

"What else," Roach said.

"What I'd give for a little rain."

"You don't like the sun?" Roach watched Miralee absentmindedly run her fingers between her toes.

"Yea, that too."

When Miralee arced her back, Roach saw her panties drooping around her thigh at the crotch. He made a note to take a pair out of the clean laundry and give them to her.

"I'll see you guys later," he said, getting off the bed, feeling the warm connective circle to Miralee seep away. Freddy nodded as he lit another cigarette. Miralee picked at some dead skin on her heel and said nothing. The baby lifted her chubby arms toward Roach and gurgled as he closed the door.

CHAPTER SIX

Though the lady at the clinic said she'd gained only twelve pounds, Mary felt as though the skin on her stomach might explode. Lying on the orange sofa, she closed her eyes and tried to pretend she was her regular size, that she could just put on her sneakers and shorts and go outside. She pictured herself skipping down Market and all the people she knew by sight sitting against the shops and the skaters doing ollies by the BART, and the old black man with the straw fedora whose name she didn't know but who used to put one hand on his heart and sing a song that had her name in it; she could see him singing it, his hand rising with the song, and Mary clutched the sides of the couch when she realized she'd been picturing herself in the wrong city.

She twisted what was left of her white-blond bangs

as her whole body sweated into the sofa. It might be marginally cooler on the mattress under the window, but Sofia had brought up a date the night before and the sheets were in a heap.

Mary gathered the sheets and took them to the tub. She turned on the cold water and watched the sheets balloon up and settle. She worried a little about catching a disease if she touched them. Though Sofia said she was careful, Mary knew this wasn't true; she'd heard the whispered promise of twenty extra and Sofia's reply of "Forty." Mary used one finger to stir the sheets, tilting her head to watch for blood or whatever, but the water stayed clear. She pulled the plug and watched any bad stuff go down the drain. She took the edge of one sheet and ran it over her temples and down her throat. Swimming would be good, though it seemed to be her fate to live near the ocean but never near enough to get to it. It'd been the same in San Francisco. She knew exactly the number of times her mom had taken her to the beach—three—all in the same summer two years ago, and only swimming that one time when her mom had drunk lots of beers and stripped to her nylon panties and big bra then ran with her body at a slant into the surf and immediately fell beneath the foam, so that Mary, still in her shorts, had to run in after her, and by the time she got to her, her mother was sitting up, wiping wet strips of hair from her eyes.

"One big wave, huh?" she'd said, then flopped over and began swimming out. Mary called for her to wait, but her mother didn't, she was thirty feet ahead, the sun reflecting crazily on the water, the tips of the wavelets molten orange. Mary had caught up and together they kept swimming toward the Golden Gate Bridge. When they stopped, Mary was amazed how quiet it was, just little plips from the waves and the swish of their arms treading the water. Kneeling by the tub, she remembered it had been late when they got out, only a few people on the beach walking their dogs. Mary had been cold and wanted to wear her mother's velour sweatshirt with the lavender teddy bears, but didn't ask because they were having such a peaceful day.

Roach whistled up to the loft. He looked down the boulevard; no one was around yet.

Mary popped her head out the window. "Hey."

"Whatcha doing?"

Mary shrugged.

"You want an ice cream or something?"

Mary pulled her bangs into a little Mohawk. "Nnn, that's okay."

Roach looked down the boulevard again, then up at Mary. "What pregnant lady doesn't want ice cream? Come on."

They stood under the whirring air conditioner of the Falafel King, licking soft-serve cones.

"Seen Dean?" Roach asked.

Mary shook her head; she hadn't seen him since he left the loft. She'd phoned his sister, who Dean sometimes called if he got picked up, but her number had been disconnected.

Roach nodded. "He's probably fine."

"Mm," Mary said, and frowned at her ice cream. She wasn't sure if she wanted Dean to be fine. The last time she'd asked him to come to the clinic, he stared at her without speaking, then slowly lowered his fist to in front of his face, where he examined it, turning it this way and that, which transfixed Mary enough that she was not prepared. Not that he landed the punches but still, he did not stop until Mary had curled over herself saying sorry, she was sorry.

"Don't you like it?" Roach asked, seeing that Mary's cone had dripped halfway down her arm.

"No, I do," she said, and started to lick herself.

Dean was a half-block up Wilcox in a one room apartment above the shoemaker's that belonged to this photographer lady named Mona who dealt pot and sometimes gave Dean money because, she said, he had "model potential," and also because he let her suck his cock. It was about the only time Mona shut up. Dean didn't know what she was talking about half the time, like when she pulled out this big book of black and white photos of sand dunes that didn't seem so great to him but which she talked and talked about, and one time started crying about, though the next morning he'd seen it lying open on the floor next to a spilled ashtray.

Her apartment was okay. Dean dug what he was doing now, waking up, smoking a joint, Mona slinking around clicking her camera at him.

"People tell you, you look like Jesus?" she asked.

"You do. Every time." He inhaled the smoke and held it. "Thinking about shaving the 'stache."

Mona clicked. "Shave it, and I won't let you up here."

"Yes you will." He rolled over and picked up the plastic clock. "I gotta split."

She put the camera on her desk. "Why don't you stay a little longer?" She started unwrapping a new pack of cigarettes. "You could take a shower."

Dean looked at Mona. He knew what she wanted but there was no way, not in the daylight. "I might come back later," he said.

Mona's smile made creases in her thin cheeks. "You have important things to do today?"

Old cunt. "I don't have to come back."

"No," she said, and took her purse off the chair. "You need a few dollars?"

Dean didn't answer.

"You want to know what I think?" she said, sitting on the futon and running her hand through his hair. "I might bring your photos to a friend of mine today."

"Yeah?" Dean tried to put some distance between himself and her breath. He just had to hold out until she coughed up, even a ten.

"Yeah," she said. "Maybe he'll put you on a billboard."

"For a car ad or some shit?"

Mona smiled, pulling the sheet down past his waist. He pressed his hands on the gray roots in her black straw hair and looked across the apartment, at the grimy toaster oven by the sink, thinking he might get five dollars for it.

CHAPTER SEVEN

Mary was watching soap operas with Sofia and MeeMee when she felt the crotch of her army pants soak through.

"Oh god," she said, grabbing at the wetness. MeeMee's eyes got enormous and she started yelling. Sofia tried to get organized, saying they could do it here if they had to, but Mary said she didn't want to; she started to cry and said she wanted to do it in a hospital, and that she wanted Dean there. They sent MeeMee to find him, and watched TV as the contractions came on. Sofia asked Mary if she wanted anything, if she had any cravings, but Mary kept shaking her head because she couldn't talk; the small of her back felt as though someone were beating on it with a tire iron. At one-thirty, MeeMee came back and said she couldn't find Dean, but she did bring Roach, who gave Mary a yellow flower and said that George, who owned the Falafel King, had agreed to give Mary a ride, but it would be better if they could do it at four, when his brother came on shift. Could she wait? She didn't know, and asked Roach to find Dean.

Sofia and MeeMee ate the food George sent up and watched talk shows while keeping an eye on Mary, asking her about a hundred times if she needed anything. Mary kept shaking her head and staring at the TV, clutching the flower and intermittently letting out moans that made the girls nervous. At 3:30, Roach came back saying he was sorry but Dean was not around, but that George was ready to take Mary. He put his arm around her and helped her down the stairwell and into George's car, and MeeMee asked, shouldn't Mary be taking some stuff to the hospital? Mary was half in the car and didn't know what to do; Sofia said never mind, they'd get stuff later, and got in with Mary. Roach stayed, saying he didn't like hospitals, and they made the drive down to County General, where Mary delivered a girl early the next morning, in a room with five other laboring women and a doctor and a nurse who said little.

Sofia waited downstairs for someone to come tell her it had happened but no one did. When she finally asked at the nurse's station, she was told she could not see the mother unless she was family, but could view the baby in a room where the lights were so dim all she could see through the window were bundles of blankets.

Sofia snorted some crank in the ladies room of the hospital before she got back in the car with George, who'd stayed in the waiting room during delivery. She talked nonstop on the drive back to Hollywood, thinking George, who was pretty old, must be fixating on how sexy she was, and waiting to see if and when he was going to pull over, which he did, in the parking lot of a place with a giant donut on top. He switched off the ignition and took a handkerchief from his pocket.

"You want coffee? I need coffee," he said, and began blowing his nose and rotating his handkerchief-covered fingers in his nostrils. Sofia opened her door and heard a tiny clink; the vial of crank was on the pavement, brown glass all broken up in the white powder. She stared at it for so long, trying to figure out how to get it back together, that George asked if she were all right; she said she was fine, to just get her a Coke. As he walked away, she pressed her palm on the speed and glass and carefully closed her hand, knowing she couldn't do it all right now. She looked toward the donut shop; the sun striking the front window made it a blinding silver. Sofia thought she could get in and out without George seeing her, and walked quickly across the lot, opened the donut shop door, grabbed a napkin dispenser off a counter, and walked back to the car, ripping out paper napkins with her teeth. She dusted the speed and glass off her palm and into a napkin, made a tiny bundle, and was sniffing what was left on her fingers just as George got in the car. He handed her a giant soda.

"I also got you a glazed," he said.

Sofia picked tiny morsels off the donut and put them in her mouth; they were like meals in themselves. Getting down the Coke was almost impossible; her throat was completely dry and felt no wider than a straw, and even if she could get the soda down she didn't know if it would stay down. When George asked again if she were okay she nodded and said she had a headache, which she did, and leaned her forehead against the cool window and stared at the city going by until they were back in Hollywood, Sofia wishing the trip had taken longer.

Mary didn't want to name the baby; she wanted to wait for Dean to come, but when they released her the following evening there was no one to meet her. The Falafel King was closed and she didn't know where else to phone, so she signed the papers with her last name, and picked the first name Angelyne and set out for the bus back to Hollywood.

She had to stop to rest three times, carrying the baby and the bin of baby stuff the hospital gave her. Getting onto the bus she thought she was going to pass out. That's when her milk came in, and it hurt so much she started to cry. Two Mexican women sitting across from her watched.

"Bena qui," one said to her, but Mary didn't know what that meant, and the other held Mary's hand and told her what to do.

The women moved to either side of her. One spoke soft Spanish to the baby and the other told Mary what to do; she must get in the shower when she got home and run the hot water on her teetas and push, and that will get out some of the milk. Also, when the baby is little like this, feed her when she wants, and later feed her every three hours. Mary nodded and used the tissues the women gave her and let the one who spoke English hold and pat her hand.

Then the bus was slowing, the women were gathering their bags, and Mary felt like the ground was falling from beneath her; she thought about picking up the baby and the tub of stuff—or just leaving the tub—and following the women off the bus. Maybe just for a few days, if they could just show her. The bus stopped, the women got off, and the one who had held her hand nodded from the top step and said, "God bless." Then she was off the bus too and the bus was moving away.

Mary took the bottom of the baby's blanket and brought it to her mouth and cried. She cried and breathed into it, and it was halfway soaked through and Mary was crying out loud now in the back of the empty bus, not thinking about the baby, only about how she wished one of the women, the one woman, would have taken her home.

At the hospital she'd phoned her dad, who she hadn't spoken to in three years, and told him she'd had a baby. All he said was, "What are you, fourteen? Jesus Christ," and then, "I hope it ain't one of those half-breeds," because he was in the military and was weird about minorities, even though his new wife was Filipina or something. He asked if Mary was calling for money, and if she was, she could forget it; why didn't she call that drunk of a mother of hers? Standing at the end of the hall in a hospital gown that didn't quite close in the back, Mary listened to her dad's hard breathing as she tried to figure out how he didn't know her mother was gone, thinking she had time to tell him before the quarters in the phone ran down, but didn't.

When Mary got to the loft there wasn't anyone around except this small Mexican kid named Pinky, whose dirty black hair clung to his scalp like a cap; he was about twelve, and because he never talked everyone thought he was halfway retarded. Mary told him he could help by making sure the baby didn't roll off the bed while she went to the bathroom.

Mary was scared when she found blood in her panties, then remembered the pads the nurses had given her. She pulled a stiff washcloth from the gooseneck pipe under the sink and rinsed it and wiped herself, then called to Pinky to bring her the sanitary napkins. A minute later the door opened a crack and Pinky's hand placed the pack of pads on the edge of the tub, a move so mouse-like and tender Mary's inhalation hooked in her throat. She was peeling the adhesive strip off the napkin when the baby cried. Mary froze; maybe she was being too loud. She peeled the paper as silently as she could. The baby howled.

Mary found Pinky patting the air a few feet above the baby. She sat on the bed next to Angelyne, whose thrust-up arms trembled with each cry. Mary touched her little finger to Angelyne's gum; the baby immediately clamped down and sucked. Mary smiled and looked at Pinky, who was stepping lightly from foot to foot. She told him everything was okay, and he walked backward to a far corner of the loft, where he crouched and began rocking.

Mary heard voices. Moving directly from sleep to the heavy fluid pressure in her crotch, Mary thought, I hope they're not tweaking, but it was only MeeMee and this mulatto fag named Guy, who had an egg-shaped head and looked like a tall, skinny girl.

"Let me see." Guy gently picked up the baby, touching his nose to hers. He had experience with babies, he said, because his sister down in Long Beach had one the year before; he even changed Angelyne's diaper while MeeMee got sloppy and cried. Mary felt her body relax. She let MeeMee fix up the mattress, and sat up in bed and drank a paper cup of hot tea that MeeMee made Pinky run out and get. MeeMee said they should wrap up Angelyne and take her out to show her off, but Guy said no, that newborns had to stay indoors at least a month, which no one at the hospital had told Mary. MeeMee asked if Mary minded if they left, and Mary said no, she was fine, and lay down with Angelyne snug in the crook of her arm, gently dabbing at the drool that collected at the corners of the baby's mouth. She thought she would fall asleep when the baby did but instead Mary ran her finger along the contours of the baby's face, petted the whorl of white-gold hair, inspected a tiny toe nail, so tiny she wasn't sure it was there.

Mary woke up to the sound of the door opening and pulled the blanket over the baby. Dean was standing by the refrigerator, looking at her.

"Come see," she said.

"In a minute." He pulled a tea towel off the counter and covered his shoulders. Mary pushed herself off the mattress, wincing through the sharp pain between her legs, and carried the baby over to him.

"See." She unwrapped the blanket.

Dean closed his eyes. "I gotta lie down," he said, then slouched away and fell onto the mattress.

Mary watched him kick at the cover MeeMee had

spread for her. The baby felt heavy in her arms as she crossed back to the bed and laid her head on Dean's chest; he didn't resist. Hearing his heart, she imagined a force circulating through him to her to the baby and back; it had a shushing sound, like in a movie she'd seen in fifth grade showing blood coursing through veins, the blueness holding cells that grew and split and made a froth, the whole thing moving constantly and keeping the heart alive, and the miracle of this filled Mary with so much faith she started to cry without making any noise until she heard Dean's breath change and knew he was asleep. The coursing ceased. Mary turned on her back and stared as the ceiling whitened, wishing it would not get light so soon.

CHAPTER EIGHT

The baby wanted to eat at eight, and again at ten, and her crying woke everyone in the loft. When Dean said something about finding a different place to get some goddamn sleep, Sofia told him he was a jerk, that it was his baby.

"Yea, maybe," he said.

Mary felt seized and knew the more mean things Dean said, the more she'd be paralyzed. Since she told him she was pregnant he'd said mean things on purpose, and when he was drunk he kept her awake with the same stories about how his father had experienced prejudice because he was Lebanese or something; that in his own country his father would have been the head of the tribe, a chief, that was why so many women wanted him, but Dean's mother wasn't smart enough to accept this and that's why she left.

"And you're no better, you don't fucking care," Dean would say, tipping off into sleep but always jerking awake and starting again with the stories, while Mary tried to keep her eyes open, even after he passed out, because her mother had told her about drunks choking on their own puke while they slept. So she didn't say anything when Dean said that about the baby, but when Roach and Top Jimmy came in right after, she got tears in her eyes, good tears. Roach's hair was messy and he looked as though he'd just woken up, but he gave Mary a hug and told her the baby was beautiful, and Top Jimmy pulled out half a cigar for Dean, who lit it and decided to be happy.

"Bring my baby over here, girl," he said real loud, and Mary did, handing her to Dean while Sofia took the cigar out of his mouth and said it was time for a celebration. Dean suggested Disneyland, which they all knew was a financial impossibility, so MeeMee suggested the Beverly Center and it was decided.

Roach and Top Jimmy didn't come; Mary didn't want to go, either, as she knew it meant shoplifting and someone would get in trouble. But she didn't want to disappoint Dean, so she sat with everyone else at the back of the bus, where the exhaust smell was strongest, and where Dean and Sofia snorted something Sofia had rolled in a napkin.

Riding up the chrome escalator, trying to keep the baby wrapped in the hospital blanket, Mary felt as though her chest would cave from the effort it took to breathe. She looked at Sofia, ahead of her on the escalator, chewing the insides of her lips.

"What do you want, Mary, what do you want?" Sofia's eyes were banging off the window displays. Mary stood in the center of the concourse and looked at the expensive stores; at Guy, mincing ahead a few feet; at MeeMee, telling him, "That's right, you fine." At Pinky, ten feet back, walking without lifting his feet. She hadn't seen where Dean had gone.

"I don't know," Mary said, watching three tall teenage girls in plaid school jumpers walk toward her. Their straight, shiny hair framed their faces as they slowed to stare at the baby, and then up at Mary. The baby started to cry, and the girls opened their mouths, and Mary saw their teeth were phosphorescent white. She tried to back away but it was as if she were mired in sludge; everything was slowing down.

"What you bitches staring at?" MeeMee planted herself in the girls' path. "You ain't never seen a baby? They ain't got no crying babies in Beverly fucking Hills?"

The girls took quick steps away, their heads huddled, the glossy hair of one slipping over her shoulder as she glanced back at Mary and flashed her teeth again.

"That's right, walk on. Whoa!" MeeMee stopped in front of a window full of Victorian dresses. "This